Published by
Penguin Books USA Inc.,
375 Hudson Street
New York, New York 10014

Produced by
Twin Books
15 Sherwood Place
Greenwich, CT 06830

© 1992 The Walt Disney Company

ISBN 0-453-03025-4

Printed in Hong Kong

10 9 8 7 6 5 4 3 2 1

WALT DISNEY'S
THE SORCERER'S APPRENTICE

Twin Books

Once upon a time, there was a clever sorcerer who practiced his magic in a workshop beneath his castle. One of his favorite magic tricks was to create a bat out of smoke, then transform it into a beautiful butterfly.

While the sorcerer worked on his magic, his apprentice, Mickey, was doing another kind of work. Day in and day out, Mickey carried heavy buckets of water up and down the stairs. He would much rather be learning how to cast spells, but his master had yet to teach him.

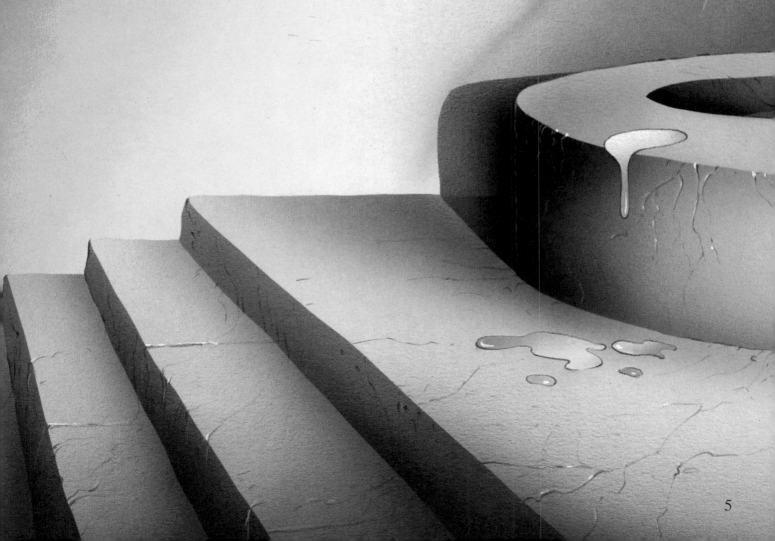

In amazement, Mickey watched the sorcerer conjure up a butterfly. The sight of the huge, floating creature made Mickey even more upset about having to do chores all day. He was convinced that he would be good at magic, if only the sorcerer would let him try.

As Mickey watched, the sorcerer fluttered his fingers, and the butterfly crumbled into a thousand pieces. The colored fragments fell into an old skull, and a bright light flared up inside it. Tired from making magic all day, the sorcerer gave a big yawn. He took off his hat and placed it on a table.

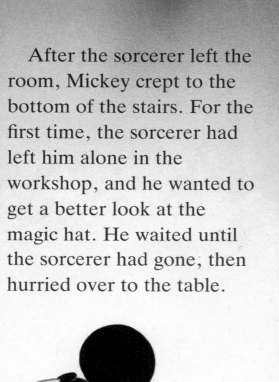

After the sorcerer left the room, Mickey crept to the bottom of the stairs. For the first time, the sorcerer had left him alone in the workshop, and he wanted to get a better look at the magic hat. He waited until the sorcerer had gone; then hurried over to the table.

Balancing on his toes, Mickey reached up and grabbed the hat. He placed it on his head, certain that it would give him the same powers as the sorcerer.

Mickey strode over to a
broom. He concentrated
with all his might, trying to
bring the broom to life.

Suddenly the broom
twitched. Arms sprung from
its sides, and the broom
stood straight, ready to obey
its new master.

Thrilled with his new powers, Mickey ordered the broom to take the buckets upstairs to the fountain, fill them with water, then march downstairs and dump the water into a big tub. He made sure that the broom understood that it had to keep filling the tub.

Satisfied, Mickey slumped in the sorcerer's chair, planning to direct the broom from there. But within moments, the apprentice dozed off. Soon he began to dream of himself as a great sorcerer, even more powerful than his master.

He dreamed that he rose
through the heavens, floating
to a place where he could
command the universe to
obey his every whim.

In his dream, Mickey
perched on a high mountain
and guided the stars across
the sky. As they streaked
past him, he ordered the
comets to follow, until the
heavens were ablaze with
light.

Then Mickey directed the waves to rise about him, higher and higher until they crashed against the rocks. As the sea spray cascaded over him, he imagined that he was the center of the universe and there was no limit to his powers.

As the water rose up, he felt his sleeves getting wet. Suddenly Mickey woke up. The workshop was flooded, and the water was all the way up to his elbows! While the apprentice had been sleeping, the broom had been working away, filling the tub until it overflowed.

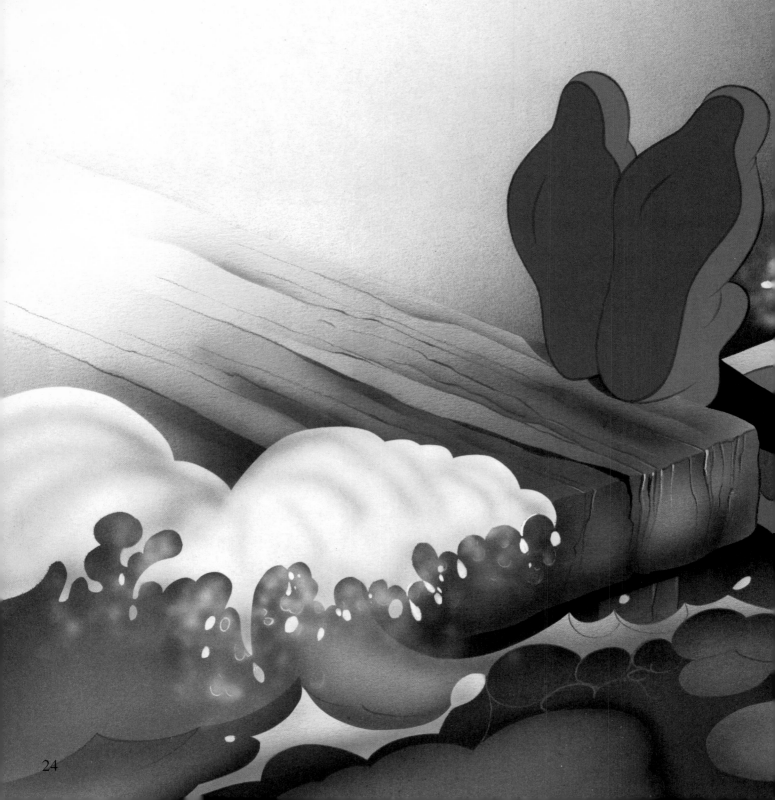

Mickey tried to get the broom to stop, but it was no use. Like a robot, the broom kept going up and down the stairs, filling the buckets and dumping the water into the tub.

Fearing that the sorcerer
would return at any
moment, Mickey grabbed an
axe and ran after the broom.
He hated to destroy the
servant he had created, but
he saw no other way to stop
it from flooding the room.

The apprentice raised the axe above his head, then brought it down on the broom. With a great *crack!*, the broom split into a dozen splinters. Tired and relieved, Mickey turned to survey the damage.

The moment Mickey
turned his back, the splinters
grew into full-sized brooms,
each carrying buckets.

Terrified, Mickey shut the
door on the brooms. But
when he peered through a
crack, he saw that they were
still advancing.

They continued to march
up to the door, then
knocked it open. The poor
apprentice was thrown to the
floor, and as he struggled to
get up, he was sorry he had
ever borrowed the sorcerer's
hat.

Soon the waves sloshed up
to the stairs. Mickey grabbed
a bucket and began
desperately bailing water. It
seemed as though the
brooms were multiplying,
and every time Mickey
tossed out some water, an
entire line of brooms tossed
in much more.

Suddenly Mickey was carried away with the flood. As he fought to stay afloat, he saw the sorcerer's magic book bobbing nearby. Quickly he leaped aboard and began searching for a spell that would stop the brooms.

But before he could find the formula, the water began to spin him around in a whirlpool. Mickey clung to the book, waiting for the water to crash down on top of him.

Suddenly a great silence fell upon the workshop. At the top of the stairs stood the sorcerer, staring at the destruction he saw below. Raising his arms high above his head, he parted the water. With another movement, he made the water disappear, until the room looked as it had before.

Ashamed, Mickey reached up and lifted the magic hat off his head. With a woeful expression he held the hat out to his master, hoping that the sorcerer would not send him away.

The sorcerer snatched the hat from him. Quickly
Mickey grabbed two buckets and gave his master a
guilty, embarrassed look.

Returning to work, the apprentice tiptoed past the sorcerer. Then, just when Mickey thought he was safe, the sorcerer swatted him with the broom – which is just what the apprentice deserved!